# To the Em$^3$ bunch

Published by Dash & Keys Publishing
Jersey City, NJ
929.269.3512
dashandkeyspublishing.com

First edition

ISBN-13: 978-0-9893633-5-8

# Queen Baby

Written by
G. Valerius

Illustrated by
Ani Bushry &
Mikka Manalo

All rise for Queen Baby!

Good morning, loyal subject.

Time for the royal bath.

I need milk, your highness.

Court jesters, make
me laugh!

Arise, sir.
An important task
awaits.

It's time for the feast.

Storyteller, tell us a tale.

And now I must rest.

# The End

# From the parents of Queen Baby:

Dear readers, especially those who find themselves as the parents or caretakers of crumb snatching, tantrum throwing, absolutely adorable children: God bless you!

# Share your feedback!

Did Queen Baby make you laugh, smile, or nod your head in agreement? Whatever your experience, I'd love to hear about it. Please share your honest reviews on Amazon!

For questions or comments, please contact:
gwendolyn@dashandkeyspublishing.com

 @queenbabybook

www.queenbabybook.com